Obadiah Coffee and the Music Contest

BY VALERIE POOLE

HarperCollins*Publishers*

For Nathan

The illustrations for OBADIAH COFFEE
were done in transparent waterproof drawing
inks and Winsor & Newton watercolor paints.

OBADIAH COFFEE AND THE MUSIC CONTEST
Copyright © 1991 by Valerie Poole
Printed in the U.S.A. All rights reserved.
Typography by Elynn Cohen
1 2 3 4 5 6 7 8 9 10
First Edition

Library of Congress Cataloging-in-Publication Data
Poole, Valerie, date
    Obadiah Coffee and the music contest / Valerie Poole.
        p.   cm.
    Summary: A rigged contest promises disappointment for most of the
animal musicians at Boxwood Gardens, unless Obadiah Coffee can
unveil the culprits.
    ISBN 0-06-021619-0. — ISBN 0-06-021620-4 (lib. bdg.)
    [1. Contests—Fiction. 2. Musicians—Fiction. 3. Animals—
Fiction.] I. Title.
PZ7.P787Ob   1991   89-49548
[E]—dc20   CIP
                                                              AC

Obadiah Coffee
and the Music Contest

Obadiah Coffee could blow a saxophone like no one else. Every member of the band knew it. Shades knew it. Fazzio knew it. Claire knew it and Elmo knew it. Even the big blue delphiniums in Mama's garden knew it. When Obadiah blew his saxophone, neighbors came from all around. They clapped and sang and danced themselves dizzy.

"Obadiah," said Mama one day, "there's a music contest at Boxwood Gardens. Why don't you and your friends try for the prize?"

Obadiah and the band grabbed their instruments and ran straight to Boxwood Gardens.

They stood outside the gate and practiced.

"Simply heavenly," said two armadillos.

"They will win the prize for certain," said a lady as she brushed by a kangaroo with a violin. The flowers on her hat tickled his nose and he sneezed—a great big sneeze.

"Bah! Flowers!" he grumped.

Obadiah and the band went into the gardens. A frog was playing his kettledrum.

"Hey ho, noodle ears!" he yelled.

"Oh, no! There's the frog who put the stink bugs in the principal's shoe," said Elmo.

"And swapped the air freshener in the girls' bathroom for skunk spray," said Claire. "I wonder what he's up to today."

The contest began. One musician strummed her harp and another blasted her tuba. The frog beat his kettledrum. The kangaroo played his violin, while his friends accompanied him on chimes and bassoon.

Then it was Obadiah and the band's turn. Elmo raised his trumpet. Claire put her trombone to her mouth. Fazzio lifted his drumsticks, and Shades drew back his bow. Obadiah saw the band was ready. He took a deep breath and blew into his saxophone. Nothing happened. He blew again. Again nothing happened. Then...

HONNNKEROOOOOP! A banana flew out of his
saxophone.

It hit one of the judges. Obadiah and the band were thrown out of the contest.

"A banana doesn't wind up inside a saxophone by accident," said Claire. "Someone put it there. Someone who doesn't want *us* to win the contest."

A flamingo strutted by in a fancy dress.

"Look!" cried Fazzio. "I bet that flamingo put the banana in Obadiah's saxophone."

"The fruit on her dress is plastic." said Claire. "The banana in Obadiah's saxophone was real."

Chefs were slicing up fruit for a lawn party that afternoon.

"Maybe one of the chefs put the banana in Obadiah's saxophone," said Elmo.

Then Obadiah and the band saw someone carrying a huge bundle. It was the frog.

"Aha!" cried Fazzio. "Open that sack!"

The frog flung the bundle open. "Loosen up, propeller ears. I'm delivering these bananas to the chefs," he said.

Back at the bandstand black-eyed peas shot out of a piccolo. Peanut butter glued cymbals together. Boiled squash oozed between the keys of a piano.

Suddenly Obadiah heard laughter. He crept around to the back of the bandstand.

The violinist and his friends were shaking with delight. The bassoonist was stuffing something into the cuffs of his pants. The chimes player was hiding something under his hat. And the violinist was tucking something inside his jacket.

Just then Obadiah remembered the lady with the flowers on her hat. And he remembered the violinist's great big sneeze.

The judges began to climb the steps to the bandstand to award the prize.

Obadiah ran to the garden. He tugged azaleas. He pulled clematis. He yanked jasmine. He ran back to the bandstand and hustled up the latticework.

"The winners of the contest," said the judge, "are the violinist and…"

He stopped abruptly. A bunch of flowers inched its way down from the roof of the bandstand and dangled directly under the violinist's nose.

The violinist's nose began to twitch. It began to wrinkle. His nostrils flared. And then it happened.…

An enormous sneeze burst his buttons and shook the bandstand. Bananas exploded from his jacket. The bassoonist jumped and peas spilled out from the cuffs on his pants. The chimes player tried to scramble away. His hat flew off, and strapped to his head were a jar of peanut butter and a squirt bottle of boiled squash.

"Bananas!" hollered Fazzio.

"Peas!" cried Elmo.

"Peanut butter!" yelled Shades.

"Squash mess!" said Claire. "The violinist and his pals have rigged the contest so they would win the prize."

The crowd hissed. They booed. The violinist, the bassoonist, and the chimes player hung their heads.

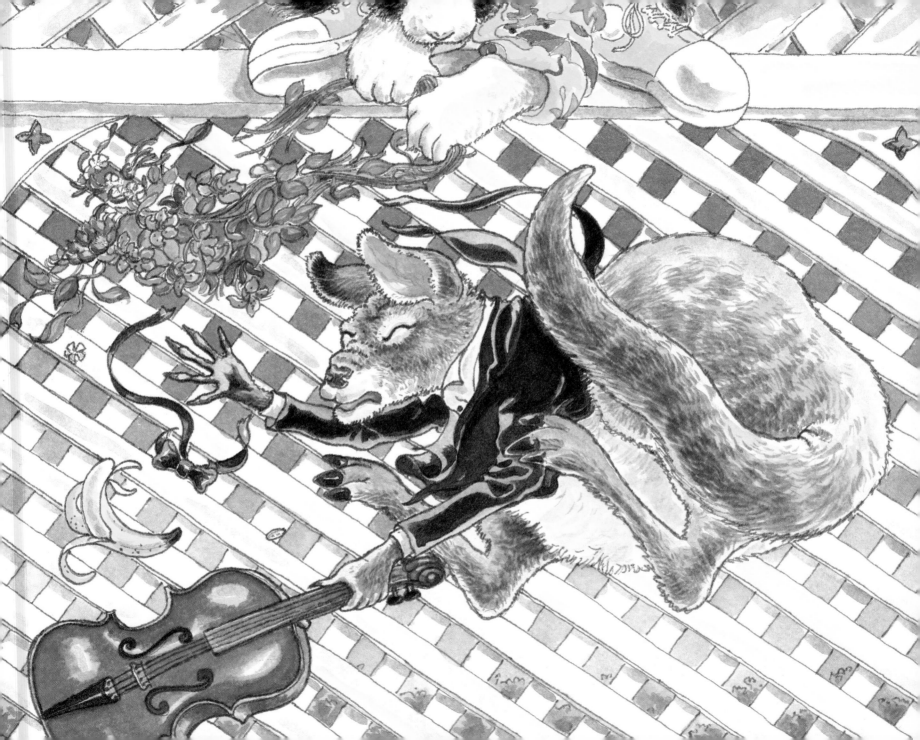

The musicians cleaned their instruments and a new contest was held.

This time when Obadiah blew his saxophone, the audience clapped and sang and danced themselves dizzy. The judges loved Obadiah and the band and gave them blue ribbons and kites.

That afternoon Obadiah and the band played for the big lawn party at Boxwood Gardens. And everyone agreed that no one could blow a saxophone like Obadiah Coffee.

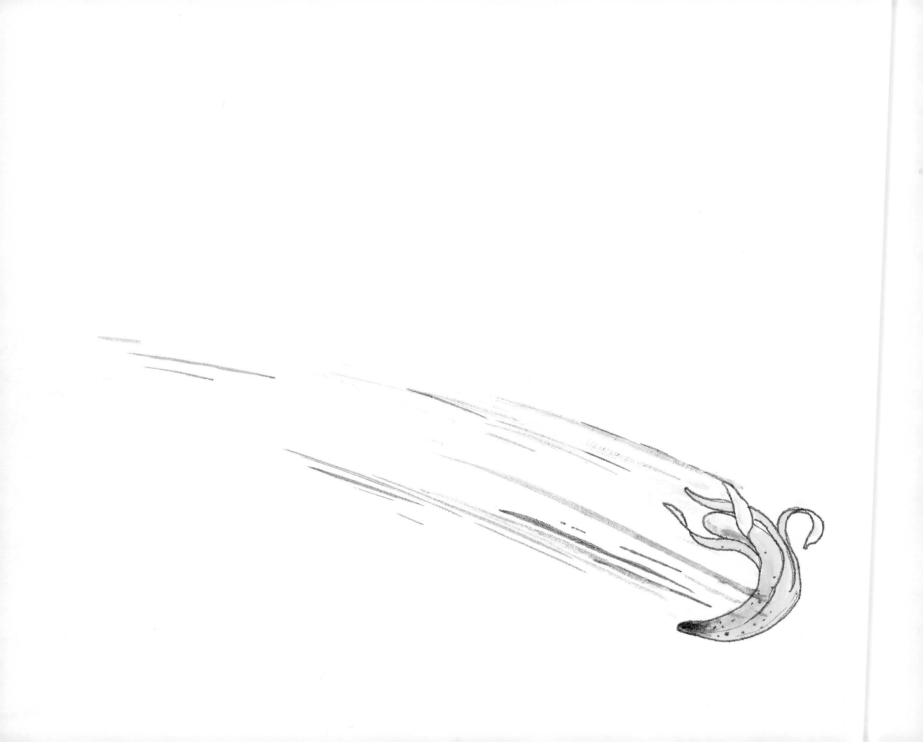